# little Miss Late

by Roger Hargreaves

WORLD INTERNATIONAL

Late for this.

Late for that.

Little Miss Late was late for everything!

For instance.

Do you know where she spent last Christmas?

At home.

Earlybird Cottage!

But, do you know when she spent Christmas?

January 25th!

One month late!

For example.

Do you know when she did her spring cleaning at Earlybird Cottage?

In the summer!

Three months late!

For instance.

Do you know when she went on her summer holiday last year?

In December!

Six months late!

Earlybird Cottage was just along the road from where a friend of hers lived.

Little Miss Neat.

Little Miss Neat was out for an evening stroll last October when she looked over the hedge of Earlybird Cottage.

Miss Late was in the garden.

"Hello," called out little Miss Neat. "What are you doing?"

"I thought I'd cut the grass!" replied Miss Late.

"I think," remarked little Miss Neat, looking at the grass, "that you should have thought about that last April!"

"Tell you what," suggested Miss Neat. "Let's go shopping together tomorrow!"

"Good idea," agreed Miss Late.

"I'll meet you in town on the corner of Main Street tomorrow afternoon," said Miss Neat.

"Two o'clock!"

"I'll be there," replied Miss Late.

The following afternoon little Miss Neat stood on the corner of Main Street at two o'clock.

Waiting for Miss Late.

She waited.

And waited.

And waited some more.

Miss Late arrived.

"Sorry I'm a bit late," she apologised.

"Sorry?" cried Miss Neat. "A bit late? It's five o'clock and all the shops are shut!!"

"Sorry," said Miss Late.

And that's what happened, all the time!

It happened when Miss Late decided to take a job.

Her first job was in a bank.

But the trouble was, by the time she arrived for work, the bank had closed for the day.

Every day!

"Sorry," she said.

They asked her to leave.

It happened in her second job, as a waitress in a restaurant.

Mr Greedy came in for lunch.

He glanced at the menu.

"I'll have everything," he grinned.

"Twice!"

He was still waiting to be served at seven o'clock.

So he went home.

"Sorry," said little Miss Late.

They asked her to leave.

It happened in her third job, working as a secretary for Mr Uppity.

"I'd like these letters typed before I go home," Mr Uppity said to her.
He went home at four o'clock.

In the morning!

"Sorry," said little Miss Late.

He asked her to leave.

However, as it happened, which is often the way of things, little Miss Late managed to find herself the perfect job.

She now works for Mr Lazy!

She cooks and cleans for him.

Cleaning his house every morning.

Cooking his lunch every lunchtime.

Now.

Mr Lazy, being Mr Lazy, doesn't get up in the morning like you and I do.

He gets up in the afternoon!

And little Miss Late, being little Miss Late, is always late for work.

So she doesn't arrive for work in the morning.

She arrives in the afternoon!

And.

Mr Lazy, being Mr Lazy, doesn't have lunch at lunchtime like you and I do.

He has lunch at suppertime!

And so you see it all works very well.

Very well indeed!

Last Friday evening the telephone rang in Earlybird Cottage.

Little Miss Late had just arrived home from work.

It was Mr Silly on the telephone.

"I've been given some tickets for a dance tomorrow night," he said.

"Would you like to come?"

"Oo, yes please," said Miss Late eagerly.

"Right," replied Mr Silly.

"I'll pick you up at seven o'clock!"

Last Saturday Mr Silly walked up the path to the front door of Earlybird Cottage.

He knocked.

"Come in," called a voice from upstairs.

Mr Silly went in.

"Make yourself at home," called little Miss Late from upstairs.

"I'll be down in a minute!"

# MORE SPECIAL OFFERS
# FOR MR MEN AND LITTLE MISS READERS

In every Mr Men and Little Miss book like this one, <u>and now</u> in the Mr Men
sticker and activity books, you will find a special token. Collect six tokens and we
will send you a gift of your choice
Choose either a <u>Mr Men</u> or <u>Little Miss</u> poster, <u>or</u> a Mr Men or Little Miss
**double sided** full colour bedroom door hanger.

Return this page **with six tokens per gift required** to:

Marketing Dept., MM / LM, World International Ltd.,
PO Box 7, Manchester, M19 2HD

Your name:_____ Age: _____

Address: _____

_____

_____Postcode: _____

Parent / Guardian Name (Please Print)_____

**Please tape a 20p coin to your request to cover part post and package cost**

I enclose <u>six</u> tokens per gift, and 20p please send me:-

| Posters:- | Mr Men Poster | | Little Miss Poster | |
|---|---|---|---|---|
| Door Hangers - | Mr Nosey / Muddle | | Mr Greedy / Lazy | |
| | Mr Tickle / Grumpy | | Mr Slow / Busy | |
| **20p** | Mr Messy / Quiet | | Mr Perfect / Forgetful | |
| | L Miss Fun / Late | | L Miss Helpful / Tidy | |
| | L Miss Busy / Brainy | | L Miss Star / Fun | |

Stick 20p here please

*Please Tick Appropriate Box*

We may occasionally wish to advise you of other Mr Men gifts.
If you would rather we didn't please tick this box

---

|← 100 mm →|

ENTRANCE FEE
3 SAUSAGES

250 mm

MR. GREEDY

Collect six of these tokens
You will find one inside every
Mr Men and Little Miss book
which has this special offer.

1
TOKEN

Offer open to residents of UK, Channel Isles and Ireland only

## Mr Men and Little Miss Library Presentation Boxes

In response to the many thousands of requests for the above, we are delighted to advise that these are now available direct from ourselves,
for only **£4.99** (inc VAT) plus 50p p&p.
The full colour boxes accommodate each complete library. They have an integral carrying handle as well as a neat stay closed fastener.
Please do not send cash in the post. Cheques should be made payable to **World International Ltd. for the sum of £5.49** (inc p&p) per box.

**Please note books are not included.**

Please return this page with your cheque, stating below which presentation box you would like, to:-
**Mr Men Office, World International**
**PO Box 7, Manchester, M19 2HD**

Your name:_____

Address: _____

_____

_____Postcode: _____

Name of Parent/Guardian (please print):_____

Signature:_____

I enclose a cheque for £_____ made payable to World International Ltd.,

Please send me a Mr Men Presentation Box ☐

Little Miss Presentation Box ☐ (please tick or write in quantity) and allow 28 days for delivery

*Thank you*

**Offer applies to UK, Eire & Channel Isles only**